Peach the Circus Pup

Emily Rose

Illustrated by Alex McVey

ISBN: 978-1-7357100-0-6

For Jimmy and Peach.

Peach was a very smart dog. She loved to do tricks like sit, spin, and roll over.

But Peach could do other tricks, too. She could hold a
ball on her nose, jump through a ring of fire, and ride
on an elephant's back!

That's because Peach was a circus pup!

Peach was born on a small farm far away from the circus. When she was still just a puppy, a man adopted her and brought her to his circus in New York. He taught her lots of new tricks and gave her a spot in his show.

Children from all over the world came to watch Peach perform. Her tricks made the children smile and laugh. Peach loved making kids happy, but she couldn't help feeling that something was missing.

Each day after the circus ended, the ringmaster took Peach to her tent. Inside were a warm bed to sleep in and plenty of food.

Peach loved the circus, but she was lonely in her tent. Being all alone made her very sad. Every night she dreamt of having a real home—one where she did not have to sleep alone and had a real friend to play with.

One day, Peach noticed a boy in the stands. His smile was bigger and his cheers louder than any of the other children.

The next day, the boy came back. And the day after. Every day for a week, the boy sat, watching Peach, his cheers growing louder each time.

Making the boy so happy made Peach happy. She began to look forward to seeing him, and saved up all her best tricks until he was in the audience.

One day after the show, Peach decided she had to meet the boy who kept coming back to see her. She went outside and began to look around for him.

Peach didn't have to look far. The boy was just outside her tent.

Wagging her tail, Peach sat down in front of him, blocking his way.

"Mom, look!" the boy shouted. "It's Peach! Hi, girl. I love your show. You are just the smartest dog there is!"

Peach jumped and did a flip, then licked his hand and sat down again. The boy laughed.

"My name is Jimmy. I just moved to town with my mom. I haven't made any friends at school yet, but I love to come watch you do your tricks!"

"We have some time before dinner, Jimmy," his mom said. "Why don't you two go off and play for a while?"

Peach wagged her tail, and Jimmy and Peach ran around the circus grounds, playing fetch and chasing each other.

Jimmy and Peach played until they were very tired.
When they came back, they found Jimmy's mom
talking to the ringmaster.

"Ah, Peach, there you are," said the Ringmaster. "And you must be Jimmy. My boy, I must tell you, Peach has been moping around here for a long time. I hate seeing her so sad. In all the time she's been living here, I have never seen her so excited and happy as she's been since you started coming to the circus. I love to see her this way, and I want her to be happy. So I must ask, would you like to bring Peach home to live with you?"

Jimmy looked nervously at his mother, who smiled and nodded. Then, squealing with joy, Jimmy shouted, "YES!" as loud as he could. He jumped up and down in excitement.

Peach was happy, too. She loved playing with Jimmy. He was fun and kind. But she did not want to quit the circus. Peach loved putting smiles on all the children's faces. It was what she was good at, and she did not want to give it up.

Peach whined and looked sadly at Jimmy.

"What about her shows?" asked Jimmy. "Will she still be able to do her tricks here for the other kids?"

The ringmaster chuckled and said, "I would like to make you a deal. As long as you promise to take care of Peach, feed her, and bring her back to the circus to do her shows every day, she can go home with you every night. You can even come to watch her every day after school if you want? Do we have a deal?"

Jimmy looked at Peach. "Do you want to come live with me, Peach? I promise to take care of you and be your best friend forever."

To answer his question, Peach ran in a circle around Jimmy, barking and wagging her tail.

"That looks like a yes to me!" said Jimmy's mom.

Peach walked home with Jimmy and his mom that very night. The next morning, he took her back to the circus so she could do what she loved: perform and make children smile. And in the evening, he brought her home again.

Day after day, Jimmy and Peach played together. Jimmy laughed all the time, and Peach loved to make him smile.

Each night before bed, Jimmy whispered, "Peach, I love you."

Then Peach licked his hand to tell him that she loved him, too.

Peach was a circus pup. But now she was a best friend, too. She had found the life she'd always wanted, and she was very happy.

The End.

CPSIA information can be obtained
at www.ICGtesting.com
Printed in the USA
JSHW021733221020
8976JS00001B/1